On the Road with

NEW KIDS
ON
THE BLOCK!

On the Road with

NEW KIDS ON THE BLOCK!

By Nancy E. Krulik

SCHOLASTIC INC.
New York Toronto London Auckland Sydney

Acknowledgments

The author would like to thank the following people for their help in researching this book: Ellen White, Stevieh Grahlnich, Walter Crow, Pat Brigandi, Betsy Huck, and Susie Hauck.

Photo Credits

Cover photo/© 1990 J. Bellissimo; #1 photo/© 1989 H. Fahrymeyer; #2 photo/© 1990 David Elkouby; #3 photo/© 1989 Marko Shark; #4 photo/© 1988 Neil Calandra; #5 photo/© 1990 David Elkouby; #6 photo/© 1990 Ken Franckling; #7 photo/© 1990 David Elkouby; #8 photo/© 1990 R. Corkery; #9 photo/© 1988 Neil Calandra; #10 photo/© 1989 Marko Shark; #11 photo/© 1989 H. Fahrymeyer; #12 photo/© 1989 Al Tielemans.

ISBN 0-590-44301-1

12 11 10 9 8 7 6 5 4 3 2 1   0 1 2 3 4 5/9

Printed in the U.S.A.   40

First Scholastic printing, August 1990

Contents

1.
Are You Ready for Show Time?

The lights in the arena go down. The audience feels the excitement. It won't be long now!

The announcer's voice blasts from the speakers: "Are you ready for show time?! Welcome, please, the five hardest working kids in show business! Let's hear it for New Kids on the Block!"

The roar of the crowd is deafening! The sold-out crowd leaps to its feet! The New Kids rush onto the stage!

When the guys ask their favorite question, "Are you ready to party?" the room rocks with the sound of 20,000 kids screaming back, "YES!!!"

Joseph McIntyre, Donnie Wahlberg, Danny Wood, Jonathan Knight, and Jordan Knight are the New Kids on the Block! Every New Kids fan has her or his own favorite New Kid. But all New Kids fans will agree on one thing — together, the fab five put on the most movin' and groovin' show in rock and roll!

The New Kids make beautiful music. Their

1

voices shine on slow, sweet ballads like their number-one hit "I'll Be Loving You Forever." And no one can rock like the New Kids can on songs like "Hangin' Tough" and "You've Got It (The Right Stuff)." But while the harmonies on their hit records may be wonderful, the place the New Kids really shine is in concert.

Maybe that's because the New Kids are happiest when they're onstage.

"The best part about being famous is being onstage in front of 20,000 people every night," Joe says. "I love hearing all the girls screaming."

And boy, do they have a lot to scream about! As any Blockhead will tell you — and only the superest New Kids fans can be called Blockheads — there's nothing like a New Kids on the Block concert. New Kids concerts are like giant sing-alongs. Everyone in the audience knows all the words to the New Kids' hits. It's truly awesome to hear 20,000 voices all join Joe in a chorus of "Please Don't Go, Girl." When they sing with the guys, the audience really becomes the newest New Kids on the Block!

There's more to a New Kids concert than the music. There's the dancing, too! The boys make up all of their own dance steps — with the help of their choreographer, Tyrone Proctor. They do some mighty fancy footwork onstage. Not just dancing, but flips and leaps, too! Donnie often complains that his ankles hurt after running around on the stage all night!

The guys can really work up a sweat when they dance. Jordan needs five towels for every show — just to wipe the perspiration from his face!

But not all the dancing at a New Kids concert takes place on the stage. Usually the beat of the Kids' music has their fans dancing in the aisles!

The New Kids on the Block want to make every person in their audience feel special. Even though the guys in the group are singing to huge crowds in giant sports stadiums, just a tip of Jordan's hat or a wink of Danny's eye can make any girl feel like her favorite guy is singing just to her!

Some nights that dream really comes true for one very lucky girl. If Donnie's feeling in a friendly mood, he might just pull a girl out of the audience. Then he'll get down on one knee and sing "Cover Girl" while he's looking right into her eyes! Wow!

From the opening notes of "My Favorite Girl" to the last notes of "New Kids Groove" and "Hangin' Tough," every New Kids on the Block show is a fun party to remember. But it takes a lot of hard work to make it all look so easy. To find out what it takes to make a New Kids show tick, let's go On the Road with New Kids on the Block!

2.
All Aboard the New Kids Express!

Most pop stars are used to traveling. When they are on tour, pop groups zigzag across the country on airplanes and buses. But the New Kids spend more time traveling than just about any other group in rock and roll. And according to statistics, the Kids probably spend one hundred times more hours a year traveling than the average person! The New Kids like to brag that they've been to forty-nine of the fifty states, not to mention Europe and Japan! When you're on the road that much, you really need to have someone around you can trust to make the road trips run smoothly.

Lucky for the New Kids, they have someone terrific to do just that. His name is Peter Work, and he is the New Kids on the Block road manager.

According to Donnie, New Kids on the Block could never put on a show without Peter. "We depend on Peter to really get things together,"

Donnie explains. "He does a great job; he's so organized. Any other group couldn't be this organized unless they had a guy like Peter as road manager."

It's Peter's job to see that the New Kids and their concert equipment are *where* they should be *when* they should be. Peter's the one who makes sure all the boys are on time for their rehearsals and sound checks. On the days the New Kids are traveling, Peter's the guy responsible for getting everyone awake and ready to go at six o'clock in the morning. That early hour is the time the group's tour buses roll in to take them to the next town!

The New Kids travel from city to city in three tour buses. Jon and Jordan share one bus. Donnie, Joe, and Danny are on the second. Peter Work travels on the third bus, along with the New Kids' bodyguards, Biscuit and Robo, and Joe's school tutor, Mark O'Dowd.

Joe is the youngest New Kid and the only one still in school. So when the boys are on the road, Joe has a private tutor to help him keep up with his schoolwork. There's no escaping homework — even if you're a superstar!

When the New Kids were just starting out, everyone traveled together in one bus. That first tour bus was a real rolling disaster! As Jon tells it, "When we first started to tour with Tiffany, we had an old bus. It kept breaking down. It was really funny. Once we had to have a tractor pull us out of the mud! Luckily things are better now."

The new tour buses are more than better. According to Donnie, they're the best!

"The new tour buses are just like home," Donnie says. "They've got living rooms, refrigerators, bathrooms, beds, and lots of things to do!"

One of the New Kids' favorite things to do on the bus is play Nintendo games. They always seem to be challenging each other on the latest video games.

"Nintendo just sent us nine Nintendo sets!" Jon says with amazement. "They are always sending us a lot of games and stuff!"

Jon used to bring his pet Shar-Pei puppy, Houston, with him on the bus. The wrinkly faced dog loved to cuddle up on Jon's lap while the boys traveled. But before long the dog got too big to be cooped up on a bus or locked up in a hotel room all day. Jon knew he wasn't being fair to his pet. It was a hard decision, but now Jon leaves Houston behind at home with his mom. The Knights have a big yard where Jon's dog can run and play all day.

As the buses roll along, Donnie can often be found watching one of his favorite movies like *Scarface* or *The Godfather* on the VCR, or sitting up front talking with the bus driver. Jordan spends a lot of time watching videotapes of Michael Jackson and Bobby Brown, just to study their dance moves. Danny tends to fiddle with his keyboards. Jon tries out new riffs on his bass, and Joe spends his time pursuing his favorite hobby — daydreaming!

But the truth is, although the tour buses have a full library of books, VCRs (stocked with all the latest movie cassettes), loads of video games, and awesome stereo systems, the thing the New Kids do most on the bus is — sleep!

"All the buses have bunk beds," Joe explains. "Most of the time we just curl up in bed and let the motion of the bus rock us to sleep."

3.
Can I Show You to Your Room?

The New Kids' tour buses pull up to the hotel in the next town sometime around ten o'clock in the morning. Peter always makes sure the group's room reservations have been made way in advance. Generally the Kids stay at the nicest hotels in town.

Although the name of the hotel the New Kids are staying at is kept secret, their fans always seem to find out where the fab five are staying. By the time the Kids' tour buses roll into town, groups of loyal fans are already waiting in the lobby to talk to them.

The boys are usually under orders not to talk to their fans in the lobby of the hotel. Hanging out with their fans could upset the other guests. But more often than not the guys will stop and sign a few autographs, anyway. Their bodyguards try to get the guys to keep moving. Joe, Donnie, Danny, and Jon tend to listen to their bodyguards. Jordan is usually the New Kid that begs to be allowed to sign just a few more.

Wherever they stay, the New Kids have to have a whole floor of the hotel to themselves. For security reasons there are guards posted at all times at every entrance to that floor. Still, some sneaky fans do manage to make their way up to the floor. Some have even gone so far as to have dressed like hotel maids to get into their favorite New Kid's room. Of course these fans are always found out, and a security guard has to escort them downstairs.

Jordan sometimes tells a story about the time he thought he caught a fan sneaking around on the New Kids' floor. He was certain the girl was following him to his room! Jordan quickly dashed down the hall and locked himself in his room. Sure enough, the girl finally knocked on Jordan's door. Imagine Jordan's shock when he discovered the "fan" was really a reporter sent to interview him. Boy, was his face red!

Money was tight when New Kids on the Block were first starting out. Sometimes all five boys had to share one hotel room. Today, the boys are worldwide superstars and each guy has his own room. Reporters and other lucky visitors to the New Kids' rooms usually have to make their way through the piles of dirty socks, fast-food containers, and candy wrappers that are all over the floor. Like most kids' rooms, the New

Kids' hotel rooms can get really sloppy!

Jordan likes staying in hotels so much, he has his own collection of hotel keys from the rooms he's stayed in!

Joe takes the easy way out of packing and unpacking in different hotels across the country. "I love touring," he says, his bright blue eyes smiling. "And I don't mind living out of a suitcase . . . as a matter of fact, I never unpack!"

While they are on tour, the hotel is one of the few places where the Kids can relax. By having a whole floor to themselves, the boys are free to wander around from room to room without being afraid of being jumped by screaming fans. The hotel is the place where the guys can finally let down their guard and get silly. And boy, do they like to get silly! Sometimes, when Danny and Donnie pass each other in the hallway, they will suddenly grab each other and start play-wrestling on the carpeted floor. Once in a while the boys have been known to break into full-scale, room-to-room water fights — just to cool down before a show.

But that's about the most mischief the Kids make in the hotels. They never, ever, wreck hotel rooms like other pop and rock stars have been known to do. Destruction just isn't the New Kids' style.

The guys really don't get much of a chance to hang out in their hotel rooms. And although they might gather in one room to watch a movie or talk before a show, what little time they do spend in the hotel is usually spent sleeping (Jon and Jordan nap the most); eating a hamburger, French fries, and a milk shake from room service; or taking a quick shower. Then it's off to the theater to start getting ready for the next show!

4.
Putting It All Together

The day of a New Kids concert is a busy one. The New Kids and their crew all work hard to make sure that evening's show will be their best show ever!

On the morning before a show the New Kids order a quick meal from room service. They don't have much time to eat, since they usually have to leave their hotel by eleven o'clock. They travel in rented limousines to the theater for a morning rehearsal.

This isn't always as easy as it seems. Fans often try to catch a glimpse of their favorite guys before they go off to rehearsal. Some of the more daring fans have even been known to climb on top of moving limousines to get the boys' attention. That's a pretty dangerous stunt! So, for the safety of the fans as well as the Kids, Peter Work usually arranges for the guys to sneak out a back door (such as through the hotel kitchen or laundry) and into the waiting limos.

Once the guys arrive safely at their destination, they get right to work. The boys run through most of the songs they will be singing in the show. According to Joe, it really isn't all that hard for the guys to decide what to sing.

"We usually do the hits," he explains. "After that we throw in the fast ones — the ones we know will make them scream!"

Besides practicing their singing, the boys make up a lot of their funky dance moves at these morning rehearsals.

"We've kind of revised the old dances [from groups like the Temptations and the Jackson Five]," Jon says of the New Kids' dancing style. "We all have good ideas for dances, and we put them together with help from our choreographer, Tyrone Proctor."

The Kids' fancy flips and bopping break-dancing moves may look easy, but they take a lot of practice. After all, when it comes to dancing, timing is everything. If one Kid is out of step, the whole number is ruined. So the New Kids rehearse the same dances over and over again until they have them down pat.

But don't be fooled into thinking that all the dancing at a New Kids show is planned and practiced. The guys' freewheeling performance style leaves them plenty of room for making up new steps right there on stage, if the mood suits them.

The rehearsal wraps up at about one o'clock in the afternoon. After a quick lunch, the New Kids are whisked over to a local mall or record store for an afternoon publicity visit. Sometimes these autograph-signing sessions are scheduled so close together the boys have to eat their lunches in the limo on the way.

"Usually during the day we're doing about a zillion things," Danny says, "like photo sessions, or signing autographs, or rehearsing, or doing interviews. The work never stops, but we don't mind it."

It's rare, but sometimes the Kids actually have the afternoon off. Then they get a chance to see the city they are playing in. And sometimes, one lucky fan gets to play tour guide!

"Every now and then you meet a fan you really click with," Joe says. "And it's nice, because she can show you around."

While the Kids are off signing autographs, giving interviews to reporters, or maybe seeing the local sights, the rest of the New Kids' crew is back at the theater getting everything ready for their show.

Robert Coleman, the Kids' wardrobe master, spends his day making sure the Kids' costumes are ready to go for that night's performance.

As soon as the New Kids come offstage after a show, they change and give their clothes to Robert. Each piece of clothing has to be checked for damage (hopefully no one has split his pants that night!) and fixed before it is packed up.

One of the first things Robert does when the group gets to a new city is unpack all the trunks of costumes. Then he and his staff search out a laundromat and a dry-cleaning store. Robert has to make sure all of the costumes are cleaned and pressed in time for the show. The Kids make at least two costume changes during a show, not counting all the hats they wear. Robert certainly has his hands full keeping track of all that clothing.

At the theater or sporting arena where the show will be performed, the stage crew spends the day taking care of the instruments and microphones. Each instrument played by the New Kids' backup band has to be set up, hooked up to an amplifier, and tuned. It's even one crew member's job to make sure the microphones smell nice!

In every city the New Kids play, the catwalk that the Kids climb out on for the "Hangin' Tough" encore has to be built and tested for safety. Nobody wants any of the Kids or any of their fans to get hurt when the guys swing out and dance over the audience in their final number.

While the stage crew is setting up the stage, the lighting crew is testing out the lights. The crew members have to check every single light bulb! Steve Glasow and Tom Krynennger, the

New Kids' laser technicians, use this time to set up their laser-light equipment and take it through a test run.

The idea for using fancy laser lighting in New Kids on the Block shows was actually Jon's. He saw the lasers used at a Debbie Gibson concert, and liked the way they worked with the music. Jon knew the lasers would add something special to a New Kids show. He was right.

At about four o'clock in the afternoon, Danny, Donnie, Jordan, Jon, and Joe come back to the theater for their final sound check. The sound check is when the boys run through part of the show, just to test out the equipment and make sure the sound is right for the concert hall. Concert halls are all built differently. The amplifiers and speakers have to be adjusted especially for the size and shape of each hall. It's the only way to make sure they sound the best they can.

The boys never just coast through their sound checks. They sing at full volume. It's the only way to make sure the sound system will be perfect when the fans get there.

"Sometimes, during the sound checks, we'll play instruments," Joe says. "Jordan's really great on keyboards; so's Danny. Donnie plays the drums. Jon's getting good on bass, and I've taken up guitar."

After the sound check, there's nothing left for

the boys to do but pile into their limos and go back to the hotel. The boys have just enough time to shower and have a little dinner. Then it is time to go back to the theater to put on a show.

For Joe, those few hours between the sound check and the concert can be pretty exciting!

"I love the buzz that develops right before the show — say about six o'clock," he says. "I get so nervous I can hardly eat!"

5.
The Opening Acts

Usually the New Kids leave their hotel to come back to the theater about an hour before they are scheduled to go onstage. That gives them plenty of time to get dressed, fix their hair, and put on their stage makeup.

While the Kids are getting ready to perform, their opening acts are already onstage, warming up the crowd. The New Kids are very dedicated to their opening acts. After all, it wasn't so very long ago that New Kids on the Block was the opening act for Tiffany.

"Tiffany remembered what it was like to be just starting out," Jon says, looking back on that first Tiffany tour. "So she gave us a break."

Many New Kids fans first discovered the Boys from Boston while they were touring with Tiffany in 1988. Tiffany's fans saw the guys at the concert and then ran out to buy *Hangin' Tough.*

"We owe her a lot," Joe says of Tiffany. "She gave us, who were a no-name group at that time, a big start."

The guys pay Tiffany back by giving their opening acts as much support in teen magazines and radio broadcasts as they possibly can. And in the case of a pal like Tommy Page, the New Kids will do even more than that!

Tommy Page is one of the New Kids' favorite opening acts. He and Jordan are such close friends that Jordan wrote a song, "I Will Be Your Everything," for Tommy to record. Jordan, Danny, and Donnie even took time off from a much-needed vacation to sing backup on the song.

"The New Kids are my best friends," Tommy says. "I can't believe they lent their talents to my records. They're the best!"

Tommy says that having the guys sing on "I Will Be Your Everything" makes up for all the practical jokes they played on him during one of their tours. One night they squirted him with water guns right onstage! Another night they pelted him with tons of stuffed animals while he was singing a soft ballad!

Tommy isn't the only opening act to have fallen victim to the New Kids' pranks. Caroline Jackson of Cover Girls recalls one of the jokes the guys played on her group.

"Once Danny and Donnie stood under our stage. They kept grabbing onto our feet so that we couldn't dance!"

The New Kids are supportive of their opening acts even when they aren't with them. Recently

Sweet Sensation took some time off from touring with New Kids on the Block to record a new album. But that doesn't mean the girls stopped hearing from Donnie, Danny, Jordan, Jon, and Joe.

"The guys always call us . . . when they're on the road," says Betty D. of Sweet Sensation. "We love to hear from them because they are such great guys!"

"We miss them when we're not with them," says Sweet Sensation's Sheila. "They're a riot. They keep us laughing!"

Oh, and by the way, Blockheads, about those rumors that Donnie and Betty are dating — Betty says that's not true. They're just pals.

Pop singer Dino is another of the New Kids' opening acts. But with hits like "24/7" and "Summer Girls," Dino may well be on his way to becoming a star in his own right. And that would be just great in Joe McIntyre's eyes. Joe is one of Dino's biggest fans.

"Dino's a really talented singer and songwriter," Joe says. "He just needs people to come out and see him. Then they'll catch on to him and like him. We're happy to help Dino. We know what it's like to be hungry."

And Dino thanks the New Kids for their support. "I couldn't have asked for more supportive guys," he says. "They really want to see my career take off, and I'm grateful."

6.
Ladies and Gentlemen, Please Welcome New Kids on the Block!

When the final applause for the opening act dies down, the New Kids know it will only be a few minutes before they have to go on! Even though the New Kids have been performing for a long time now, they still get nervous backstage.

"When the press gives our shows a lot of hype, I'll get scared [before we go on]," Danny admits.

To ease the backstage butterflies in their stomachs, the Kids take those last few minutes before they perform to prepare themselves — physically and mentally — for the show.

Donnie has his own special performing superstition. He never shaves before a show — he's convinced shaving will bring him bad luck!

Right before they go onstage, all of the New Kids drink Maurice Starr's original mixture of honey-lemon tea, just to soothe their throats. Then the Kids and Maurice Starr, the man who brought together the five New Kids, go through a special two-minute ritual that no one is allowed to interrupt — for any reason! They get together in a tight circle, hold hands, and close their eyes. Maurice says a special prayer thanking God for their talent and success. The prayer is something the boys and Maurice have done before every performance since the group's beginning.

When the prayer is over, the Kids reach up and slap each other's hands for good luck. Then they run out on to the stage and break into song!

No matter how well planned a concert may be, there's always a chance something will go wrong. That's the risk you take when you perform live. The New Kids' shows are no exception. But the Boys from Boston are real pros. When a problem occurs, they handle it without panicking!

Donnie recalls one time when the group was lip-syncing the words to one of their songs. When you lip-sync, you are really just mouthing the words to a song while a recording plays in the background. Unfortunately, at this particular performance, the record simply stopped playing!

"I suggested we sing *a cappella* [without music]. It worked out pretty well. We found out that night that we could sing *a cappella*. We'd never tried it before."

A regular problem for the Kids is taking care of their clothes. "I can't tell you how many times my pants have ripped onstage," Joe says. "But stuff like that is bound to happen."

Jon is always worried about the lighting and equipment. "We've been pretty lucky lately," he says. "But there are so many things that can go wrong."

The biggest worry is that the New Kids won't make it to the concert at all! Recently the Kids were scheduled to play at the Omni arena in Atlanta, Georgia. The night before the guys had put on a show in New York City. The day of the Atlanta show, the New Kids were stuck in a New York airport. All flights out of New York were delayed because of thunderstorms. Luckily the weather eventually cleared just enough for the Kids to fly. They arrived at the Omni just as their opening act was taking the stage!

When the guys are onstage, they give their all. There isn't a second when they aren't working hard to please their fans. Keeping up that kind of energy level is hard work. In the early days, the New Kids would finish their concerts and come offstage feeling tired and worn out. But now they are in better shape, and they finish every show feeling pumped up and awake!

After a show, most pop groups will head out of the theater as fast as they can. But not New Kids on the Block. The New Kids usually take an hour or so to hang around backstage and talk to the lucky fans who have won backstage passes in contests from local radio stations. It's just the New

Kids' way of letting their fans know how important they are!

If you are looking to meet your favorite New Kid after he leaves the concert hall you can forget about running into him at a local dance club. The New Kids just don't hang out in clubs. After a show they are more likely to go right back to their hotel and go to sleep. After all, by the time the Kids get back to their hotel, it is usually about two o'clock in the morning. And the tour buses will be outside again at six A.M., ready to take the guys to the next town.

7.
The Fans Speak Out!

The New Kids work very hard to make each show a concert their fans will never forget! Do they succeed? Here's what their fans have to say.

When Michael Nemeth went to a Tiffany concert in July 1988, he had no idea who New Kids on the Block were — except that they were the opening act for Tiffany.

"Nobody knew who they were when they announced the opening act," Michael says. "I just thought, oh, well, another one of those no-name groups. But when I heard them, well, their music really hits you! So I thought, these guys are a pretty good group. They'll probably be popular someday."

Michael was right about that. But no one could have predicted how quickly "someday" would come around.

"I never thought they would get big that quick," Michael says with amazement. "I mean, I went to that concert in July 1988, and by the time school started again in September, everyone knew who they were!"

In 1989, Michael went to another Tiffany concert. The New Kids were performing, too. But things were different this time. *Tiffany* came on first. In a few short months, the New Kids had become so popular that Tiffany had become the opening act for them!

Michael says that even without Tiffany, he would go to see the New Kids in concert again. "Their music really is very good," he explains. "And it's the age thing. It's fun to see a really popular group of young kids."

Azure O'Neil saw her first New Kids concert in March 1990. By that time, the New Kids were big stars, and everyone in the audience was there just to see them.

"The opening acts were okay," she says, "but I just couldn't wait for the New Kids to come on."

When the New Kids finally did take the stage, it was a moment Azure says she'll never forget!

"The best moment of the show was when they first came on. I just couldn't believe they were there!" she exclaims.

Azure's favorite New Kid is Donnie. So she was really excited when Donnie started to sing "Cover Girl." After all, that's the song where Donnie chooses to pull a girl out of the audience and sing

to her. Unfortunately Donnie sang to someone else, but Azure loved hearing the song anyway. "It's still my favorite," she says.

When Lauren Donato heard Joe McIntyre sing "Treat Me Right" in concert, she couldn't believe her ears. "It sent tingles up and down my spine," she says. "I'll never forget it."

Joe is definitely Lauren's favorite New Kid. "I love the way he dances . . . and he's so cute!"

Lauren has been a New Kids on the Block fan for about a year and a half. And like most New Kids fans, she collects everything that has pictures of the fab five on it.

"I have posters all over my room," Lauren says. "I have books, magazines, a New Kids watch, and lots and lots of pins."

Lauren has a special message for her favorite group. "I just want to tell them all that I love them!"

Believe it or not, a lot of girls at Jacqueline Attard's New York school don't like New Kids on the Block! But that doesn't stop Jacqueline from wearing her New Kids shirts and pins to school.

"When some of the kids see my best friend and me wearing our shirts, they make fun of us for liking the New Kids," she says. "But we wear our shirts proudly!"

Jacqueline is going to her very first New Kids

concert this year. She can hardly wait to see the New Kids live!

"I know there will probably be a lot of girls screaming through the show. But I'll probably scream, too," she admits.

Jacqueline's favorite New Kids are Joe and Danny, but she says she really loves them all. What she loves most about them is "They go around to all the schools and tell kids, 'Don't do drugs.' They have a good image. And they are really talented. Every time I listen to their songs I get all shaky!"

Amy Illingworth is a true Blockhead! She's been to a New Kids concert, she's got New Kids posters all over her room, she listens to their albums all the time, and she collects every magazine, book, and newspaper article that even mentions the New Kids.

Amy had a real close-up view of the New Kids when she saw them in concert. She had seats right on the floor of the arena! "We had to stand on our chairs to really see them," Amy says, "but that was okay. It was just so exciting to see them right there in person, up close!" Just like everyone else in the audience, Amy screamed so loud she became hoarse!

Nicole Raney got her New Kids concert tickets

as a birthday present from one of her friends. "It was a really, *really* nice birthday present," she says with excitement.

Nicole describes the night she saw the New Kids in concert as one of the best nights of her life. Her favorite part of the whole show was the finale. "I really liked when Donnie came out on the ramp that they have. I actually like Jordan the best of all the New Kids, but I liked the finale of the concert a lot. The laser lights that they flashed were really nice."

Olivia Ford hasn't been a New Kids fan for very long, but now that she's discovered the Kids, she's making up for lost time. She already has three of their albums and one of their videotapes, and she's started putting their pictures all over her room. Olivia says she likes the way the guys dance and sing, and she especially likes the words to their songs.

So far, Olivia hasn't seen the New Kids in concert, but that's not to say she hasn't tried to get tickets to one of their shows. "My friend and I were trying to win contests on the radio. But we kept missing them. We were trying to get the tickets through the contests because the show was all sold out!"

Luckily for Olivia, even though she hasn't been able to see the Kids live in concert, she has been able to watch them perform up close on their *Hangin' Tough Live!* videotape.

Hangin' Tough Live! is the best-selling music video Columbia Music Videos has ever made. Lauren Margulies, a buyer for a chain of video stores in California, thinks that's pretty easy to explain.

"The video captured their dynamic concert style," she says. "And it's much more personal than being in the audience at the concert.

"The video has almost taken the place of the teen magazines for fans," Lauren continues. "It's something you can keep. And you can watch the New Kids in concert every night!"

What a great idea!

8.
Hangin' Tough — Together!

There's no doubt that the New Kids love traveling from town to town, putting on concerts to make their adoring fans happy. Happiness is what the New Kids on the Block are all about.

"We do it for the fans," Joe says. "You can do so much. You can make a girl's day or even her year, just by shaking her hand, saying hi, or giving her a hug. That's special."

"There's nothing like seeing your fans enjoy your show to give you a big thrill," Donnie adds. "That's what we're all about!"

But the pressures of a heavy touring schedule and always having to be "up" for the fans can really force the New Kids' tempers to flare every now and then.

"Jon and I spend a lot of time together, and sometimes we get in each other's hair," Jordan admits. "But overall we've really learned a lot about each other touring together. I have to admit one thing — when we finally get home, I don't care if I see Jon. I'd rather spend time with the rest of the family. I don't get to see a lot of them."

Not seeing their families is a regret all five New Kids share. Each of the guys easily admits that he gets homesick once in a while.

"I admit that I miss my mom when I'm on the road," Donnie says. "When she shows up for a show, I can't help but run up to her and kiss her. I know it sounds corny, but she's the greatest!"

Of all the cities he's been to, Jon says his favorite is Boston, "because it's home, and home is the best place to be!"

To help ease their homesickness, the boys like to shop for presents for their families back in Boston. It's their way of sharing their success with the people they love most.

"Part of the great joy of success is sharing it with your loved ones," Donnie says.

But don't worry too much about the New Kids. The boys are like brothers. And like all brothers, they help each other when they feel sad or homesick.

"We take care of each other," Donnie says. "It's not like we'll stop each other from eating junk food, like our moms would. That's one of the good things about being on the road. We just try to make sure everyone's OK."

9.
Regular Kids on the Block

After a long and exhausting tour, there's no place the New Kids would rather go than home to Boston!

"One of the things I look forward to the most at the end of a tour is coming home and sleeping in my own bed," Joe says.

For the New Kids, doing everyday things with all of their hometown pals is another great part of being home. It's exciting to them just to be able to grab a slice of pizza at the Hi-Fi Pizza Restaurant, pick up a soda at the Li'l Peach Convenience Store, and play basketball at the Dorchester Youth Collaborative with friends from the old days. According to some of those friends, it's great having the Kids back in town, too — even if it's just for a while.

Sixteen-year-old Joanna has been friends with Joe McIntyre for a long time. Joanna's aunt and one of Joe's sisters are close friends, so Joanna and Joe are close friends, too. When they were

33

both little, Joanna and Joe went to Florida together with their families. Through her pal Joe, Joanna has gotten to know all five of the New Kids on the Block.

Joanna's got good news for New Kids fans. She says the guys are really every bit as sweet as they seem onstage.

"When they are onstage they're just themselves," Joanna says. "They're not going up there and showing off."

According to Joanna, even though the New Kids are the same sweet guys they always were, people in the Boston area sure treat them differently now.

"Joey tried to come to a dance at the high school last year. But there were all these girls there who started screaming, and Joey had to leave," Joanna explains. "I wouldn't want to talk to Joe around other people anymore. No matter where he goes people are always screaming."

Joanna says that because fans camp outside their homes, all of the New Kids have security guards watching their houses now. The Kids even have to hide their garbage!

"If there's garbage lying around the fans come and dig through and take stuff — just because they think one of the New Kids has touched it," Joanna says, laughing. "Can you believe it! Someone even took Joe's mailbox!"

Although the New Kids love seeing their fans, having them hang out around their homes is another story.

"They worry about their families," Joanna says. "Some of them have had to put up high fences around their houses."

All of this has been hardest on Jon Knight. All of his life Jon's been an avid gardener. It has always been relaxing for Jon to go outside and do some planting or weeding in his garden. But some fans once tore a tiny tree he planted for his mother right out of the Knights' yard. And now, every time he walks out into the garden the girls go crazy. So Jon spends most of his days at home inside with his tropical fish tanks.

It is almost impossible for any of the New Kids to go anywhere without being chased by adoring fans. Last year the Kids visited Faneuil Hall, a place in Boston that's filled with restaurants and shops. Lots of Boston teens hang out there, and before they were stars, the New Kids did, too. In fact, Faneuil Hall was always one of Jordan's favorite places to shop for his funky outfits. But when the Kids went to Faneuil Hall last summer, the police had to come to hold back the crowds!

So now, when the New Kids want to relax with their Boston buddies, they usually do it at private parties. Only the New Kids' closest friends are allowed to come to the parties, so the guys are sure they'll be treated like one of the gang. Joanna is one of the lucky friends who has been invited to a few of the New Kids' private parties.

"At the private parties, nobody treats them any differently," Joanna explains. "It's just good friends getting together and having a good time."

Of course the New Kids don't always hang out together when they're home. They take the time to see friends and family they don't get to see while they are on tour.

"They hang out together sometimes, but they all have their own crowd of kids," Joanna says. "Remember, they aren't all the same age, and they went to different high schools."

That's true. Donnie and Danny both went to Copley High School. Jordan and Jon went to the Thayer Academy. Joe was a student at Catholic Memorial High School.

Surprisingly enough, Joanna says that before they became famous, the guys in New Kids on the Block weren't particularly popular at school.

"They were pretty much all normal kids," she says. "Like, take Joe. I wouldn't say Joe was top rank or anything, but he had friends."

Still other people who went to school with the New Kids say that the guys weren't popular at all. In fact, some kids thought they were pretty strange.

"People thought it was really weird that Jordan

Knight and Danny Wood were always going out break dancing instead of hanging out with everybody else," says one classmate of Danny's at Copley High School.

Of course now nobody would think the New Kids were anything less than totally cool! But as the Kids' real friends will tell you over and over again, the Kids haven't changed. The attitudes of the people around them have.

Bill Foley has been a friend of the McIntyre family for many years. He has known Joe's parents since before Joe was born. Bill says stardom hasn't changed the youngest New Kid a bit.

"You know, Joe always liked the stage," Bill says. "He's been acting since he was two. He's always had talent, so this success comes as no surprise. It feels great to see him become famous. He's the kind of kid who always shares his success.

"Just yesterday I saw Joey taking his mother out for dinner. He'd rented a Mazda sports car to take her out in."

Bill is proud that Joe is a singing superstar. And he's proud that Joe hasn't changed because of his fame. But the thing about Joe that Bill is most proud of is the fact that he has kept up with his schoolwork.

"He travels with a tutor, and he's even taking a few college courses," Bill says. "He knows how important education is."

One of the things the New Kids like to do when they come home is play basketball. "They'll go down to the school and shoot baskets," Bill says. "They'll sign autographs for all the kids who play basketball at the school. What can I tell you — they really are just regular kids on the block!"

10.
What's New for New Kids on the Block?

You would think that all the touring the New Kids on the Block do would keep them too busy to do anything else. But the New Kids aren't called the five hardest working kids in show business for nothing. They are always thinking up exciting ways to keep their fans happy!

The first thing on the fab five's schedule is finishing up the work on their new album, *Step by Step*. It's scheduled for release in the summer of 1990 — just in time to make every Blockhead's summer super sunny!

Step by Step is the group's fourth album. Just like the songs on *New Kids on the Block*, *Hangin' Tough*, and *Merry, Merry Christmas*, the music on the Kids' latest album is written almost entirely by Maurice Starr. Usually Maurice produces all the songs on the New Kids' albums, too.

The big change on the new album is that a few of the songs have been written and produced by a songwriting, engineering, and producing group called The Crickets. Surprise! The Crickets are really Donnie, Danny, and Jordan.

The New Kids have been working on *Step by Step* since November 1989. How could they have been touring and recording at the same time? Simple — the guys recorded most of the album in between concerts!

During their last tour, the New Kids' manager, Dick Scott, sent recording equipment up to the Kids' hotel rooms. The guys recorded the vocals right in their rooms. The instrumental music was recorded by musicians back in Boston. The boys' vocals will be mixed with the recorded music for the final album. The boys had hoped to play the instruments on the new album themselves, but there just wasn't time.

Step by Step is filled with beautiful ballads and dynamite dance tunes. "I can guarantee you one thing," Joe says about the new album. "I don't think anyone will be disappointed. The music will be a lot of fun!"

But that's not all, Blockheads! Starting in September, you'll be able to see New Kids on the Block on your TV every Saturday morning! The New Kids on the Block TV show will be a mix of live action and cartoons. At the start of each show the boys will introduce the cartoon. At the end of the show they will perform one of their hit songs. In between the introduction and the song there will be a cartoon adventure featuring animated New Kids. But listen closely to the voices of the cartoon Kids. They're soundalikes, not the real thing. The New Kids really wanted to record their own voices, but they just didn't have the time in their schedules to do it. Hey, there're only so many hours in a day, and the guys have lots to do!

While you are watching the fab five on TV, look for TV commercials featuring those living dolls, the New Kids on the Block, and the new plastic dolls that look just like them! Hasbro toys has created a whole line of fashion dolls that look just like Donnie, Danny, Joe, Jordan, and Jon.

"When I first saw the dolls I thought, 'Gee, that's really bizarre,' " Jon says. "But after a while I thought it was pretty cute. You know you've really made it when they model a doll after you."

The New Kids are already being featured in commercials for Coca Cola, too.

In October 1990, the Kids will try their hands at acting. They are scheduled to go in front of the cameras to begin filming their very first movie! Nobody knows when the movie will be in the theaters, but keep your eyes out for it.

And as if a full-length New Kid movie weren't enough, come Christmastime the boys will be taping a holiday special for prime-time network television! That's the best Christmas present any Blockhead could ask for!

In addition to their group projects, some of the individual New Kids have projects of their own.

Donnie is producing a rap group. The group's called Northside Posse, and it is made up of some of Donnie's high school buddies. Donnie hopes to do for Northside Posse what Maurice Starr did for New Kids on the Block.

Jordan hopes to write more songs for his pal Tommy Page and for New Kids on the Block. He's also got hopes for a solo album — but don't worry Blockheads, Jordan's not leaving the group!

Jordan and Jon are also hoping to get their adopted brother Chris and his rap group launched on their own careers. Maurice Starr is helping Chris Knight out, too — he's given him a four-track recording machine. It's the same one he used to record the early New Kids on the Block music!

How's that for a lucky charm?

11.
Fast Facts About New Kids on the Block

Fast Fact #1

Who started New Kids on the Block?

Donnie, Joe, Danny, Jon, and Jordan are five really different guys. So how did they ever decide to get together and form a rock-and-roll band?

They didn't! The truth is New Kids on the Block was really the creation of record producer Maurice Starr.

Maurice had already put together the successful group The New Edition (the group that launched singer Bobby Brown's career) when he got the idea to put together five Boston guys who could sing, dance, and rap.

In the summer of 1984, Maurice and his friend, music agent Mary Alford, started to audition boys from all over the Boston area. It took Maurice almost six months of listening to boys sing and watching them dance before Maurice decided on Donnie, Danny, Jonathan, Jordan, and Joe.

Maurice never doubted the talent of the five

boys he picked to be in New Kids on the Block. Susie Hauck, a fan of many local Boston bands, remembers meeting Maurice backstage at a New Music concert in 1986. "He was talking about this new band, New Kids on the Block," Susie recalls. "I didn't know who they were . . . [but] he kept saying they were going to be huge. He was really pushing for them, and not just with anybody. He was trying to make sure the important people knew who they were."

Maurice was right. New Kids on the Block did become a huge success and before long *everyone* knew who they were.

Fast Fact #2
Who was the first New Kid to join the group?

The first New Kid to join the group was Donnie. He'd heard about the auditions through some friends in his Dorchester neighborhood. Even though he was afraid that he couldn't sing well enough, Donnie decided to try out for the group. He gave the audition his best shot — he even did his Michael Jackson dance impression. Whatever Donnie did that day, it sure worked. Maurice Starr signed him up on the spot!

Fast Fact #3
Weren't there two other members in the original New Kids on the Block?

When Donnie went to audition for New Kids on the Block, he dragged his brother Mark along. Mark tried out, too, and both he and Donnie made the group. But Mark decided being in New Kids on the Block took too much time away from his friends and playing basketball, so he quit the group.

Donnie also asked a good friend of his named Jamie Kelley to join the group. Jamie certainly was talented enough to be a New Kid, but his parents thought he was too young for the pressures of show business.

Fast Fact #4
What was the original name of New Kids on the Block?
Would you believe Nynuck?! Nobody knows why the guys picked that name. But they sure changed it fast after people started jokingly asking "Which one of you is Nynuck of the North? Ha ha."

The name New Kids on the Block came from a rap the Kids did called "New Kids on the Block."

Fast Fact #5
Where did the New Kids play their first concert?
At a prison on Deer Island in Massachusetts. The combination of singing in his first concert and being in a prison made Jon so nervous his knees

were shaking through the whole show!

Fast Fact #6
Were the New Kids an overnight sensation?

Not unless you consider four years overnight! The New Kids spent a lot of time playing small clubs in the Boston area sharpening their singing and dancing skills.

When the Kids recorded their first album, *New Kids on the Block*, in 1986, it wasn't a big hit at all. In fact, it was a major disappointment! Their second album, *Hangin' Tough*, might have been one, too, had Tiffany not asked the guys to be her opening act. Tiffany's audiences loved New Kids on the Block, and the rest, as they say, is history!

Fast Fact #7
Have the New Kids ever been booed?

Believe it or not, New Kids on the Block have been booed by the audience twice!

The first time was back in 1984, when the boys were first getting started as Nynuck. They were playing at a Kite Festival in Franklin Park in Roxbury, Massachusetts. The boys had to do their dancing on picnic tables and lip-sync their songs to a tape. They started with "Stop It, Girl!" But before they could finish the song the audience started booing.

Finally Donnie grabbed a microphone and told

the crowd that they were going to finish their act whether the audience wanted them to or not. And by the time the Kids finished with their "New Kids on the Block" rap, the audience was cheering along.

The second time New Kids on the Block got booed was at the Boston Music Awards in 1990. They had just won an award. Donnie says he was hurt most by the musicians who booed the band out of jealousy.

"I don't get it," he says. "We support Boston bands. Even if we hadn't won, we would have been happy for the guys who did."

That's just the kind of generosity that sets New Kids on the Block above all the rest!

Fast Fact #8
Do the New Kids do any charity work?
Do they ever! The New Kids believe in giving to those less fortunate than they, and to prove it they have become the teen spokesmen for United Cerebral Palsy. The Kids donated profits from their hit single "This One's for the Children" to United Cerebral Palsy, and part of the money earned from calls made to their 900 number goes to the organization, too.

Another cause the New Kids are dedicated to is keeping kids off drugs. They have worked so hard for this cause that Massachusetts governor

Michael Dukakis named Monday, April 24, 1989, New Kids on the Block Day.

Fast Fact #9
Which New Kid shops the most?
All the new kids are into style, but it is sweet, shy Jon that does the most shopping. In fact, the other New Kids have nicknamed him GQ, after the men's fashion magazine *Gentlemen's Quarterly*.

Fast Fact #10
Which Kid gets the most fan mail?
Jordan gets the most letters, at least from the fans in America. In Japan, more girls go crazy over Danny than any other New Kid. All together, the New Kids get more than 30,000 letters a month!

If you want to send a fan letter to the New Kids, here is the address:

New Kids on the Block Official Fan Club
P.O. Box 7080
Quincy, MA 02269

12.
New Kids on the Block Trivia Tests!

How big a Blockhead are you? Take these terrific trivia tests and find out. (Answers on pages 53–55.)

How Well Do You Know NEW KIDS ON THE BLOCK?

1. Why are the New Kids' mothers called the Posse 30?
2. Which New Kid's nickname is Puff McCloud?
3. The video for "I'll Be Loving You Forever" was taped at a school in what borough of New York City?
4. Which New Kid isn't from Dorchester?
5. What is the name of Jon's dog?
6. Which New Kid's good-luck charm is his stuffed animal, Tigger?
7. How many awards did the New Kids get at the American Music Awards in January 1990?
8. When they toured Japan the boys made com-

mercials for what Japanese company?
9. Which New Kid is allergic to cats?
10. Who is the only New Kid with blue eyes?

How Well Do You Know JORDAN?
1. True or false: Jordan is the baby of the Knight family.
2. Which of the following is Jordan's favorite book? a. *Charlotte's Web* b. *Jonathan Livingston Seagull* c. *Frankenstein*
3. Where was Jordan born?
4. Which ear does Jordan have pierced? a. right b. left c. both
5. True or false: Jordan chews on his ponytail when he gets nervous.
6. Is Jordan right- or left-handed?
7. What is Jordan's full name?
8. What instrument does Jordan play?
9. What is Jordan's nickname?
10. When is Jordan's birthday?

How Well Do You Know DONNIE?
1. True or false: Donnie's ponytail is really a fake hair weave.
2. True or false: Donnie is afraid of roller coasters.
3. What is Donnie's favorite cereal? a. Lucky Charms b. Raisin Bran c. Count Chocula

50

4. In the *Hangin' Tough Live!* video, what does Donnie's shirt say?
5. What astrological sign was Donnie born under?
6. How many brothers does Donnie have?
7. What instrument does Donnie play?
8. Which of the following is Donnie's favorite saying? a. Peace Forever b. Peace Out c. Peace Now
9. What does Donnie always wear around his neck?
10. When is Donnie's birthday?

How Well Do You Know JOE?
1. When was Joe born?
2. What is Joe's favorite TV show?
3. Where was Joe born?
4. What is Joe's favorite sport?
5. True or false: Joe was the first guy to join New Kids on the Block.
6. What blue-eyed performer is Joe's favorite singer?
7. What is the name of Joe's oldest sister?
8. True or False: Joe does impressions of the other New Kids all the time.
9. Which of the following is Joe's favorite kind of food? a. Chinese b. Italian c. Mexican
10. What does Joe wear around his neck?

How Well Do You Know DANNY?
1. True or false: Danny wears glasses.
2. What is Danny's favorite sports team?
3. What kind of pets does Danny have?
4. What is Danny's middle name?
5. What are the names of Danny's folks?
6. What college did Danny leave to go on the road with New Kids on the Block?
7. What was the first record Danny ever bought?
8. When is Danny's birthday?
9. What does Danny try to do whenever the group arrives in a new town? a. look for an Italian restaurant b. go to a mall c. scout around for the nearest gym.
10. What kind of earring does Danny wear?

How Well Do You Know JON?
1. True or false: Jon actually prefers to be called Jonny.
2. What is Jon's favorite food?
3. What is Jon's full name?
4. What is Jon's nickname?
5. True or false: Jon's favorite kind of music is heavy metal.
6. True or false: Jon is the oldest New Kid.
7. What are Jon's favorite colors?
8. When is Jon's birthday?
9. True or false: Jon likes McDonald's burgers the best.
10. What color are Jon's eyes?

ANSWERS to NEW KIDS quiz

1. Because between them they have 30 children.
2. Danny
3. Brooklyn
4. Joe — he's from Jamaica Plain.
5. Houston
6. Danny
7. Two; one for best pop group, and one for best pop-rock album. Way to go, New Kids!
8. Sony
9. Joe
10. Joe

ANSWERS to JORDAN quiz

1. True
2. b
3. Worcester, Massachusetts
4. c
5. False. He bites his nails.
6. Left-handed
7. Jordan Nathaniel Marcel Knight
8. Keyboards
9. "J"
10. May 17, 1970

ANSWERS to DONNIE quiz

1. True. He usually has it cut out when his mom visits.
2. False. He's afraid of Ferris wheels.
3. c

4. Homeboy
5. Leo
6. Five
7. Drums
8. b
9. His peace medallion
10. August 17, 1969

ANSWERS to JOE quiz
1. December 31, 1972
2. *Cheers* ('cause it takes place in Boston!)
3. Needham, Massachusetts
4. Golf
5. False. He was the last. Donnie was the first.
6. Frank Sinatra
7. Judy
8. True
9. c
10. His confirmation medallion

ANSWERS to DANNY quiz
1. True — but never when he's performing.
2. Basketball's Boston Celtics
3. Goldfish. Their names change from week to week.
4. William
5. Elizabeth and Daniel
6. Boston University
7. *Let's Dance* by David Bowie

8. May 14, 1970
9. c. Danny likes to lift weights and work out as much as possible.
10. A gold G-clef

ANSWERS to JON quiz
1. False. He really likes to be called Jonathan best of all.
2. Chocolate chip cookies
3. Jonathan Rashleigh Knight
4. "GQ"
5. False. He prefers rhythm and blues.
6. True
7. Black and white
8. November 29, 1968
9. False. He prefers Burger King's.
10. Hazel

A MAP TO THE NEW KIDS' HANGOUTS

Maurice Starr's House
Jordan, Jon, Danny, Donnie, and Joe first auditioned for New Kids on the Block at Maurice's Roxbury home.

Copley High School
Danny and Donnie both went to Copley High.

Li'l Peach Convenience Store
Joey used to hang out in front of the Li'l Peach, and dream about stardom with some of his Jamaica Plain pals.

The Dorchester Youth Collaborative
You can still catch the New Kids at the DYC. When they're home they love to play basketball there with their friends.

Hi-Fi Pizza Restaurant
Donnie says it's got the best pizza in the world!

St. Thomas Church
Joe first fell in love with the stage when he played Oliver Twist in the Boston Neighborhood Children's Theater production of *Oliver!* The group rehearsed in this church.